When Dragons Fly South for the Winter

Written and Illustrated by

Judy Sorrels

To Isla & Aubrey,
Enjoy the dragons!
:) Judy

judysorrelsart.com - publications

judysorrelsart.com
judysorrelsart publications

When Dragons Fly South for the Winter

First edition, published 2021

Written and Illustrated by Judy Sorrels

Copyright © 2021

Hardcover ISBN 978-0-578-95956-6

Dedicated to my kids,
Catherine and Michael, who inspire
me in so many ways. To my husband
Mark, who is my rock,
and first and foremost, to God.

It starts when the
very first snowflake,
floats lazily down
from the sky.

and lands on the nose

of the

tiniest dragon.

The signal!

That's it!

Time to FLY!

They pack in a hurry and flurry,

their snorkels, and flip-flops and such.

Each dragon takes only their favorites.

Those baskets don't hold very much.

No dragon stays home for the winter.

Their toes get too cold in the snow.

They don't have snug hats or warm mittens,

so they're happy when it's time to go.

Where do those sun-loving dragons,

fly southwards to? Where do they go?

To avoid all the brrs,
and the wintertime grrs,
and forget about
shoveling snow?

When dragons fly south for the winter,

they take all of their summery things,

stuffed tightly in bright colored baskets,

as they joyfully take to their wings.

They land on the warm, sandy beaches,

where they wiggle their toes in delight.

The little ones leap off their dad's giant backs.

Let's play, it was such a long flight!

Please blow up the beachballs, set up the big net!

We're ready to play in the sand, and get wet!

On goes the sunscreen.

Can you please get my back?

I see some big fishes!

Thanks, mom,

yummy snack!

When dragons
play out in the
sunshine,
no matter how
young or how old,

their hearts get
revved up, their
fires relit,
like nothing that happens
when dragons are cold.

They share every goodie and nibble,

with a dragon-wink, nod,

and a SLURP.

They bring their own fires for toasting
marshmallows, which do make them
BURP.

At night they sing songs by the fire,

telling stories of brave deeds and wishes,

Like the time someone's dad escaped by just inches, from a school of amazingly **BIG, GIANT FISHES!**

Too soon the warm
water turns chilly.
The sun shines a little
less bright,

and the nose of the BIGGEST, BIG dragon,

sniffs the air, and just knows,

TIME FOR FLIGHT!

When dragons fly north for the summer,
they remember the songs,
and the jokes.
They look forward to
making more memories,
back home with all of their folks.

CPSIA information can be obtained
at www.ICGtesting.com
Printed in the USA
LVHW020716241021
701344LV00004B/42